Kitty Up!

by Elizabeth Wojtusik

pictures by Sachiko Yoshikawa

For Dahli Jane, because she was first—E.W.

To Nimbus—S.Y.

DIAL BOOKS FOR YOUNG READERS
A division of Penguin Young Readers Group
Published by The Penguin Group
Penguin Group (USA) Inc., 375 Hudson Street, New York, NY 10014, U.S.A.
Penguin Group (Canada), 90 Eglinton Avenue East, Suite 700, Toronto, Ontario, Canada M4P 2Y3
(a division of Pearson Penguin Canada Inc.)
Penguin Books Ltd, 80 Strand, London WC2R ORL, England
Penguin Ireland, 25 St. Stephen s Green, Dublin 2, Ireland (a division of Penguin Books Ltd)
Penguin Group (Australia), 250 Camberwell Road, Camberwell, Victoria 3124, Australia
(a division of Pearson Australia Group Pty Ltd)
Penguin Books India Pvt Ltd, 11 Community Centre, Panchsheel Park, New Delhi - 110 017, India
Penguin Group (NZ), 67 Apollo Drive, Rosedale, North Shore 0632, New Zealand
(a division of Pearson New Zealand Ltd)
Penguin Books (South Africa) (Pty) Ltd, 24 Sturdee Avenue, Rosebank, Johannesburg 2196, South Africa
Penguin Books Ltd, Registered Offices: 80 Strand, London WC2R ORL, England

Designed by Kimi Weart
Text set in Walters
Manufactured in China on acid-free paper

Library of Congress Cataloging-in-Publication Data

Wojtusik, Elizabeth.
Kitty up! / by Elizabeth Wojtusik ; pictures by Sachiko Yoshikawa.
p. cm.
Summary: A lively little Kitty has an outdoor adventure that ends with a rainstorm and her rescue by Big Dog.
ISBN 978-0-8037-3278-0
Special Markets ISBN 978-0-8037-3423-4 Not for Resale
1. Cats—Fiction. 2. Dogs—Fiction. 3. Stories in rhyme. I. Yoshikawa, Sachiko, ill. II. Title.
PZ8.3.W8185684Kit 2008
E dc22   2005016197

The art was created using acrylics and pastel on illustration board.

This Imagination Library edition is published by Penguin Group (USA), a Pearson
company, exclusively for Dolly Parton's Imagination Library, a not-for-profit
program designed to inspire a love of reading and learning, sponsored in part by The
Dollywood Foundation. Penguin's trade editions of this work are available wherever
books are sold.

Kitty up.

Kitty down.

Kitty square.

Kitty round.

Kitty fast.

Kitty slow.

Kitty stop.

Kitty go!

Kitty leap!

Kitty still.

Kitty won't.

Kitty will!

Kitty hunt.

Kitty creep.

Kitty drowsy.
Kitty sleep.

Kitty cozy.

Kitty dream.

Kitty wake.

Kitty scream!

Kitty lost.

Kitty peek.

Kitty gasp.

Kitty shriek.

Kitty listen.

Kitty hear.

Kitty hope.

Kitty cheer!

Kitty lucky.

Kitty friend.

Kitty home.

Kitty end.